Grammie's Secret Cupboard

by Cynthia Furlong Reynolds
illustrations by Bert Dodson

mitten press

All inquiries should be addressed to:

Mitten Press

An imprint of Ann Arbor Media Group LLC

2500 S. State Street

Ann Arbor, MI 48104

Printed and bound in China.

10   9   8   7   6   5   4   3   2   1

Library of Congress Cataloging-in-Publication Data

Reynolds, Cynthia Furlong.
Grammie's secret cupboard / by Cynthia Furlong Reynolds ; illustrations by Bert Dodson.
p. cm.
Summary: A young girl discovers her true talent when her grandmother looks deep into her
eyes, then opens a hidden cupboard and selects a special plaything just for her.
ISBN-13: 978-1-58726-310-1 (hardcover)
ISBN-10: 1-58726-310-6 (hardcover)
[1. Grandmothers--Fiction. 2. Individuality--Fiction. 3. Self-esteem--Fiction.] I. Dodson, Bert,
ill. II. Title.
PZ7.R33513Gra 2007
[E]--dc22
2006035738

Book design by Somberg Design
www.sombergdesign.com

This book is dedicated to
the memory of
Esther Henley Leighton
of South Portland, Maine (1897–1972),
a grandmother who lived a life
of unconditional love.

"Did you know that Grammie has a secret cupboard?" my cousin Jeffrey whispered to me. "She keeps special toys there—one magical toy for each kid—and no one else will ever play with it."

Could that really be true?

"A secret cupboard?" I asked suspiciously.

But Jeffrey didn't answer. He just hopped onto his bike, waved, and rode off.

"Bye, Mom! Bye, Daddy! Bye, Susanne and Betsy!" I
shouted and waved as the red station wagon headed
down the street and disappeared around the corner.
Then I took Grammie's hand and skipped very happily
into the warm, old-fashioned kitchen.

After we'd helped ourselves to strawberry pie and lemonade, Grammie asked, "What would you like to do tomorrow? We have all day to ourselves!"

I didn't have to think very hard for an answer.

"I want to go to the beach! And make sand castles! And take a picnic lunch! And stick my feet in the icy cold water! And dig for pirate treasure!"

"Then that's what we'll do," Grammie promised with a hug.

HNOH! HNOH! HNOH!

The sound of the foghorn woke me from dreams of sand castles and egg salad sandwiches and Spanish treasure chests. Raindrops ran down the windows, and the foghorn's cries were warning ships at sea about dangerous rocks. They were also warning a little girl that there would be no Special Day.

"Grammie!" I wailed, running down the old wooden stairs and bursting into the kitchen.

"There, there, it's all right," she said, bending down to hug me. "We'll have another kind of Special Day."

Sitting on a blanket in front of the fireplace in the old-fashioned parlor, we played games. Checkers. Cat's Cradle. Jacks. Old Maid and War. Grammie played the piano, and we sang songs from the long-ago days when she was a girl. We chose pictures of furniture from Sears & Roebuck catalogs and pasted them onto a big brown piece of paper. We cut out pictures of ladies and glued them onto cardboard to make paper dolls; then we designed clothes for them. In between, we listened to the rain and foghorn.

This was fun, but it wasn't like a day at the beach!

After picking up the last scraps of paper and twisting the cap on the glue bottle, I whispered, "Grammie, right now I'm a little bored."

"Let's go to The Cupboard," she suggested.

The Cupboard?

THE CUPBOARD!!!

There really was a secret cupboard???

Next to the fireplace, a paneled wall looked like an ordinary wall, but if you knew exactly where to push your hand— like Grammie did—a hidden latch would spring a door open, revealing a secret cupboard big enough to hide a little girl.

Well, Grammie pushed, and the door snapped open! A secret cupboard!

I stood on my tiptoes and craned my neck to glimpse what was inside, but I couldn't see anything.

Grammie could, though. I heard her rustle among all the secrets. She'd stop, think, then whisper, "No..." She'd rummage a little longer, pause, and say no again.

And again.

And again.

Finally, after what seemed like forever, she gave
me my Special Toy.

The only thing was, it didn't look like a toy!

It was a book, a beautiful book. Grammie
had glued a piece of flowery wallpaper onto
cardboard to make book covers. Then she'd gathered
all kinds of different colored papers and drawn lines
on them in different colored inks. She sewed the
pages to the covers, like a real book.

But there was something wrong with this book!

"Hey! Grammie! This book doesn't have any words or pictures!" I pointed out.

"Those are for you to create," she said, handing me a sparkly pink pencil and heading toward the kitchen.

I dropped my head and whispered, "But Grammie, I don't know all my ABCs yet."

My grandmother stopped, turned, and peered at me over her glasses before she said, "I know that you have stories to tell. Write them down and come into the kitchen when you're done. I'll read your book with you."

With those words, she disappeared.

Well, I had nothing else to do, so I
started to write.
I wrote.
And I wrote.
And I wrote.
I wrote until I'd filled all the pages.
Then I marched into the kitchen that
always smelled like molasses cookies.
"My book is done!" I said proudly—
and a little nervously.

Grammie stopped mixing
and stirring, sat down on the
closest kitchen chair, and pulled
me into her lap. As I held my
breath, she looked at every
page of my book. Every single
page. Without saying one word.
   "Uh-oh!" I thought to myself.
But then she began to read.
She read.
And she read.
And she read.

She read a story about the adventures of a little girl my age who had an older brother—I'd always wanted an older brother! There were pirates—I loved hearing about pirates! And adventures on sailing ships! And treasure chests! And then, just when my heart was pounding so fast and I thought, "They'll never get out of this trouble!!" there was a happy ending.

The ending came at the very bottom of the last page.

After Grammie closed my book, we sat in the cozy kitchen, listening to the crickle-crackle of the fire in the old stove, the drops raining on the roof of the old house. Neither of us said a word for a very long time.

Finally, I had to ask. "Did I write that story?"

My grandmother smiled when she hugged me. She looked deep into my eyes and said, "You're going to be a writer when you grow up!"

"Yes, I will!" I promised.

From that rainy, foggy day onward, I never doubted it.

Many years later, when we were all grown up, Grammie's seventeen grandchildren gathered on her front porch to remember her and her secret cupboard. I told my story and then my sisters and cousins chimed in with their own stories about Grammie's magic.

From out of the cupboard my sister Susanne had been given rolled balls of woolen cloth and lessons on rug braiding; she grew into a gifted textile artist. My sister Betsy and my cousin Melinda received doctor's kits; nowadays they work in the world of medicine. My sister Joy inherited Grammie's love for baking; she and her husband create magic in kitchens. That pesky cousin Jeffrey (who grew up to become a very fine man!) was given a set of tiny, intricate blocks; he works on real homes nowadays.

"Let's see what's in the cupboard now," Cousin Martha suggested that day when we all were sitting on Grammie's porch. We rose to follow her. But my mother—who is as wise a woman as her mother was—stopped us.

"That's Grammie's secret cupboard. Do you really want to spoil the magic?" she asked.

We thought for just a moment. Then we all returned to our seats on the porch, leaving the secrets of the cupboard to the special moments in our past.

I don't know if I became a writer because Grammie saw some clue about my future within me, or because she gave me permission and encouragement to become whatever I wanted to become. But I do know that the world would be a wonderful place if all children had a special person to look deep into their eyes and discover the magic there.